Grandfather
Tang's Story

Grandfather

Crown Publishers, Inc.
New York

Tang's Story

Ann Tompert

Illustrated by
Robert Andrew Parker

Grandfather Tang and Little Soo were sitting under a peach tree in their backyard. They were amusing each other by making different shapes with their tangram puzzles.

"Let's do a story about the fox fairies," said Little Soo. So Grandfather Tang arranged his seven tangram pieces into the shape of a fox.

Then Grandfather Tang made another fox with Little Soo's seven tangram pieces. Little Soo clapped her hands as her grandfather began.

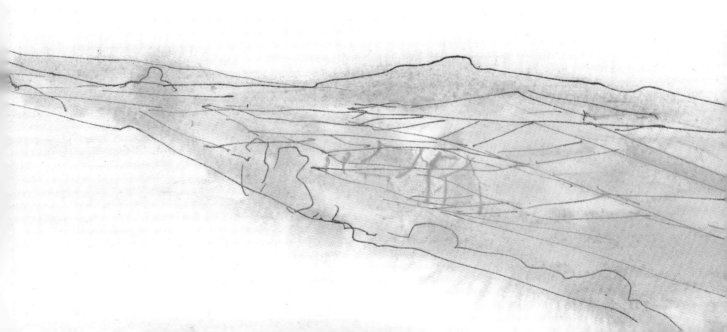

Although Chou and Wu Ling were best friends, they were always trying to outdo each other. One day this rivalry almost brought their friendship to a tragic end. They were sitting under their favorite willow tree beside a river talking about their magic powers.

"I can change myself into a rabbit as quick as a wink," boasted Wu Ling. "I'll bet you can't do that."

"I can too," said Chou.

"Can not," said Wu Ling. "Anyway, actions speak louder than words." And he changed himself into a

rabbit.

"Not bad," said Chou, smoothing his whiskers. "But watch me do better than that."

And before Wu Ling could blink, Chou changed from a fox into a

dog!

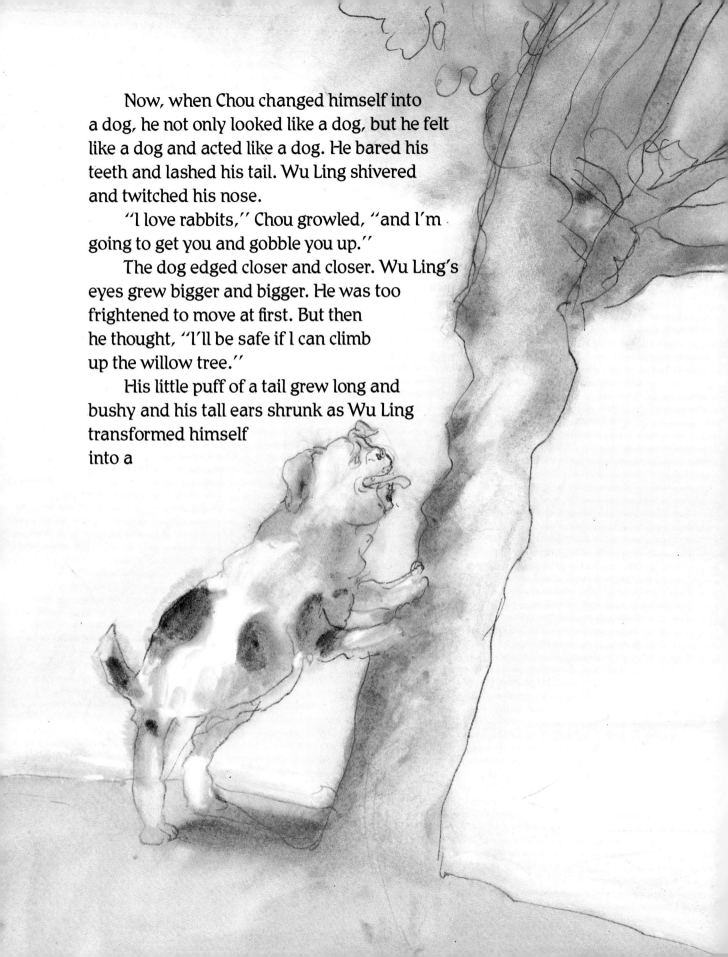

Now, when Chou changed himself into
a dog, he not only looked like a dog, but he felt
like a dog and acted like a dog. He bared his
teeth and lashed his tail. Wu Ling shivered
and twitched his nose.

"I love rabbits," Chou growled, "and I'm
going to get you and gobble you up."

The dog edged closer and closer. Wu Ling's
eyes grew bigger and bigger. He was too
frightened to move at first. But then
he thought, "I'll be safe if I can climb
up the willow tree."

His little puff of a tail grew long and
bushy and his tall ears shrunk as Wu Ling
transformed himself
into a

squirrel.

Wu Ling sprang into the willow tree and scrambled to the top.

"Chou will probably turn himself into a cat so he can climb up the tree after me," Wu Ling said to himself. "But he'll never catch me. I'll jump from tree to tree, and he won't be able to follow me."

Of course, Chou thought about changing himself into a cat.

"But that's just what Wu Ling expects me to do," he said to himself. "What can I do to surprise him?"

He thought and thought.

"I know. I'll swoop down upon him from above."

And he turned himself into a

hawk.

Chou circled round and round in the sky above the willow tree, searching for Wu Ling. Wu Ling peered through the leaves of the tree, looking for Chou on the ground.

Round and round Chou circled the willow tree until he spied Wu Ling.

"*Kek! Kek! Kek!*" he shrieked as he zoomed down upon the squirrel.

Wu Ling trembled. Chou's beak looked sharp enough to pierce right through him.

"If only I lived in a shell house," he thought. "Then Chou couldn't hurt me."

Chou stuck out his fierce claws to seize Wu Ling, but Wu Ling dove toward the river below the willow tree. And as he dove he tucked in his head and tail and legs, turned green, and changed into a

turtle.

Wu Ling climbed up on a mossy rock in the middle of the river. He thought he was safe because he looked as if he were a part of the rock. Chou circled round and round, searching and searching, until his sharp eyes spotted the turtle. Then he swooped down, down, down toward him.

But just as Chou reached him, Wu Ling plunged into the water.

"Follow me and you'll drown," he cried.

"Don't worry," cried Chou, plunging right behind Wu Ling.

His body grew longer, covered with scales. He whipped the water with his long, wicked tail. And he snapped his spike-toothed jaws as he turned into a crocodile.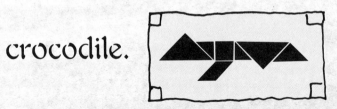

Wu Ling circled round and round as he plunged down, down, down to the bottom of the river. Chou lashed his wicked tail as he plunged after Wu Ling. Just as they

reached the bottom, Chou clamped Wu Ling in his
spike-toothed mouth.

"Now, I've got you!" he bellowed through his clenched
teeth.
"Oh, no, you haven't," cried Wu Ling, who grew
smaller and smaller and changed himself from green to
gold as he transformed himself into a

goldfish.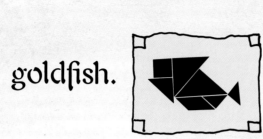

And he swam out of Chou's mouth between his spiked teeth.

Then he hid in a patch of cattails. Chou churned the water with his lashing tail as he charged into the patch after Wu Ling. With his head swinging back and forth and his eyes darting here and there, he searched for Wu Ling. Wu Ling knew that Chou would not give up until he found him.

"I must fly from here," he thought.

And he started to honk as he transformed himself into a

goose.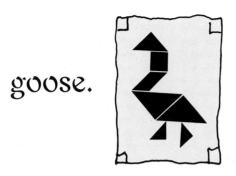

Chou charged after him, but Wu Ling spread his wings and took to the air.

Chou watched him fly to a small island where a flock of geese were feeding. By now he was not only very angry, he was also very hungry. He decided that if he could not catch Wu Ling, any goose would make him a good dinner. He splashed through the water toward the island until he reached it.

"*Honk! Honk! Honk!*" called Wu Ling.

And he took to the air.

A chorus of honks swelled the air as the flock of geese spread their wings to follow him. While Chou watched, the honking grew fainter, the flock grew smaller, and he felt his anger slowly drain away.

"Why, oh, why did we play that stupid game?" he moaned. "I'll never see Wu Ling again."

He closed his eyes and sank toward the river's bottom. Just as he touched it, however, he had an idea. And up he popped again, a goose himself.

Moments later, Chou was flying after Wu Ling and the other geese. He could hardly see or hear them at first. But he did not let this discourage him. Calling upon every last bit of his strength, he forged ahead.

Each flap of his wings brought him closer. The wedge
of geese slowly grew bigger. The honking grew louder. At
last Chou found himself flying beside Wu Ling.

"I'm tired of our silly game," he cried. "Come back with me to our willow tree."

Before Wu Ling could answer, something stung Chou's right wing. He sank toward the ground.

A hunter had shot him. Wu Ling flew down beside Chou, placed his left wing under Chou's smashed right wing, and together they fluttered down to the edge of the forest.

The hunter ran toward them.

"Fly away," Chou urged Wu Ling. "Save yourself. Fly!
Fly!"

"I won't desert you," cried Wu Ling.

And with a mighty roar, he changed into a

lion.

The hunter raised his bow. Wu Ling sprang toward him and knocked the bow from his hand. The hunter fled, leaving his bow behind.

Wu Ling and Chou returned to their fox shapes. And
Wu Ling helped Chou to his den, where he took care of him
until he was mended.

D id they ever play that game again?'' asked Little Soo.

"Many times,'' said her grandfather. "But they were very, very careful.''

"That was a good story,'' said Little Soo. "Let's do another.''

Grandfather arranged his seven tangram pieces.

"Is this story going to be about a man?'' asked Little Soo.

"Yes,'' said her grandfather. "He's old and he's tired. He wants to sit under a tree and rest awhile.''

"Is he a grandfather like you?'' asked Little Soo.

"Yes,'' said her grandfather. "Just like me.''

Little Soo arranged the seven pieces of her tangram beside her grandfather's.

"Is that a little girl?" he asked.

"Yes," said Little Soo. "Just like me. She'll sit and rest beside the man."

"That will make him very happy," said Grandfather Tang. "And now, Little Soo, what will we do?"

"We'll sit and rest together until Mother calls us for supper," said Little Soo.

"That will make me very happy," said her grandfather.

Tangrams

Tangrams are ancient Chinese puzzles that are still used today by adults as well as children.

A tangram begins with a square, which is then cut into seven standard pieces. Each piece is called a *tan*. In creating a picture, all seven tans must be used; they must touch, but none may overlap.

When tangrams are used in storytelling, the storyteller arranges the tans to show the shape of a character in the tale. As new characters or story elements are introduced, the puzzle pieces are rearranged to represent the new character or new element.

The fox fairies in Grandfather Tang's story are an integral part of Chinese folklore. They are believed to be endowed with supernatural powers of transformation. Fox fairies are said to live for eight hundred to a thousand years.

Ann Tompert became interested in tangrams when she saw some books about these Chinese puzzles in a catalog. She sent away for the books and became so intrigued by the challenge of the puzzles that she began making up her own tangrams and stories about them.

You can trace the tans on this page onto a clean sheet of paper, then cut them out to make your own tans.

For Claudia, Max, and Jack Parker — R.A.P.

Text copyright © 1990 by Ann Tompert
Illustrations copyright © 1990 by Robert Andrew Parker

Library of Congress Cataloging-in-Publication Data. Tompert, Ann. Grandfather Tang's Story / Ann Tompert ; illustrated by Robert Andrew Parker.
Summary: Grandfather tells a story about shape-changing fox fairies who try to best each other until a hunter brings danger to both of them.
   ISBN 0-517-57487-X   ISBN 0-517-57272-9 (lib. bdg.)
[1. Storytelling – Fiction.   2. Foxes – Fiction.   3. Fairies – Fiction]   1. Parker, Robert Andrew, ill.   ll. Title
PZ7.T598Gr 1990 [E] – dc20 89-22205

24 23 22 21 20 19 18 17